SHARING THE BREAD

AN OLD-FASHIONED THANKSGIVING STORY

WRITTEN BY
PAT ZIETLOW MILLER
ILLUSTRATED BY
JILL MCELMURRY

schwartz & wade books · new york

Mama, fetch the cooking pot.

Fetch our turkey-cooking pot.

Big and old and black and squat.

Mama, fetch the pot.

Daddy, make the fire hot.

Tend it so it's blazing hot.

Ready for the cooking pot.

Daddy, make it hot.

Sister, knead the
rising dough.

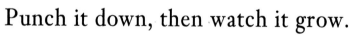

Punch it down, then watch it grow.

Line your loaves up in a row.

Sister, knead the dough.

Fetch. Heat. Knead the bread.

Work together till we're fed.

Brother, baste the turkey well.

Baste that tasty turkey well.

Such a good Thanksgiving smell.

Brother, baste it well.

Grandpa, cook the berries, please.

Boil those bright red berries, please.

Add some lemon—just a squeeze.

Grandpa, cook them, please.

Grandma, bake your pumpkin pie.

Whip the topping light and high.

High enough to reach the sky.

Grandma, bake the pie.

Baste. Boil. Bake a treat.

When can we sit down to eat?

Auntie, mash potatoes now.

Just like Grandma taught you how.

Top with butter from our cow.

Auntie, mash them now.

Uncle, swing the cider jug.

Swing that gallon cider jug.

Pour a drink in every mug.

Uncle, swing the jug.

Baby, be a sleeping mouse.

Such a peaceful, sleeping mouse.

Snug and happy in our house.

Baby, be a mouse.

Mash. Top. Pour. (And rest.)

Food and loved ones. We are blessed.

I will fold some pilgrim hats.

Proper paper pilgrim hats.

Perfect festive table mats.

I will fold some hats.

Now I'll raise a hearty shout.

A happy, hungry, hearty shout.

"COME AND GET IT!
DINNER'S OUT!"

I will raise a shout.

Family, find your dining place.

Choose a chair and fill your space.

Bow your heads and ask for grace.

Family, find your place.

Fold. Shout. Sit. Pray.

All together on this day.

We will share the risen bread.

Our made-with-love Thanksgiving spread.

Grateful to be warm and fed.

We will share the bread.

To my parents, Allen and Jean Zietlow,
who helped hone my love for food and family
—P.Z.M.

For Jennifer, Norma, Charles, Rosemary,
Isabelle, Mario, Leona, Maxine, Jim, and Gary
—J.M.

Text copyright © 2015 by Pat Zietlow Miller
Jacket art and interior illustrations copyright © 2015 by Jill McElmurry

All rights reserved. Published in the United States by Schwartz & Wade Books,

an imprint of Random House Children's Books, a division of Random House LLC, a Penguin Random House Company, New York.

Schwartz & Wade Books and the colophon are trademarks of Random House LLC

Visit us on the Web! randomhousekids.com

Educators and librarians, for a variety of teaching tools, visit us at RHTeachersLibrarians.com

Library of Congress Cataloging-in-Publication Data
Miller, Pat Zietlow.
Sharing the bread : an old-fashioned Thanksgiving story / Pat Zietlow Miller ; illustrator Jill McElmurry.
—First edition.
pages cm
Summary: Illustrations and simple, rhyming text reveal a family's preparations for their Thanksgiving feast, with everyone pitching in to help—
including Baby, who sleeps quiet as a mouse.
ISBN 978-0-307-98182-0 (trade) — ISBN 978-0-307-98183-7 (glb) — ISBN 978-0-307-98184-4 (ebk)
[1. Stories in rhyme. 2. Cooking—Fiction. 3. Family life—Fiction. 4. Thanksgiving Day—Fiction.] I. McElmurry, Jill, illustrator. II. Title.
PZ8.3.M6183Sh 2015
[E]—dc23
2014010933

The text of this book is set in Archetype.
The illustrations were rendered in gouache on watercolor paper.
Book design by Rachael Cole

MANUFACTURED IN CHINA
2 4 6 8 10 9 7 5 3 1
First Edition